Acknowledgements

Many minds, hearts, and hands contributed to bringing this story and the entire Mambo series to life. The book is written and illustrated by Africans to showcase Africa's culture out of a Design Studio in Cameroon. Special thanks to the Balafun Creative team: Blaise Pascal Tine and Franck G. Mensah.

This work is dedicated to…

To all the children—especially the "Mambos" of Africa, whose lives are a source of inspiration and whose futures can be brightened by education.

Library of Congress Control Number: 2014921748

Mambo Goes to School

Written by Gladys Kenfack
Illustrated by Hertzy O. Vital

Text and Illustrations copyright © 2014 Balafun LLC
16212 Bothell-Everett Hwy #F357
Mill Creek, WA
www.balafun.com

Printed in the United States of America

ISBN: 978-0-9908757-2-7

Second Edition

MAMBO
Goes to School

By Gladys T. Kenfack
Illustrations by Hertzy O. Vital

It's morning time! Mambo cheerfully stretches and rolls out of bed. Today is a very special day! Today, Mambo is going to school for the first time.

Mambo joins the other kids at the river for a bath. He cannot contain his excitement and says,

"I'm a big boy, and I get to go to school today!"

The village kids are happy for Mambo and wish him a fun first day of school.

After his bath, Mambo joins his mother for breakfast. He slowly eats his donuts and drinks corn porridge. Mambo is curious and anxious about school.

"Mom, what am I going to do at school? Is school fun?" he asks.

His mother smiles and says, "You will like school very much."

With teary eyes, Mambo puts on his new school uniform and packs his schoolbag. He makes sure he does not forget his lunch: a handful of ripe bananas.

Just before leaving for his big day at school, Mambo points to his dog and asks hesitantly,

"Can Rondo come with me to school?"

His mother answers, **"Dogs do not go to school, Mambo. They cannot read, write, or count."**

She then asks, **"Would you like me to come with you, Mambo?"**

"No thank you, Mom! I am a big boy, and I am going with the other kids. Have a great day!"

Mambo says as he walks toward the road.

As Mambo joins the line of students walking to school, he meets his friend, Kai. Both Mambo and Kai happily skip to the village school.

Soon, Mambo and Kai arrive at school. The tall man at the bell invites them to take part in the First Day of School Ceremony by the flag pole.

The ceremony takes place under a tree. Mambo volunteers to lead the students in the singing of the national anthem. After the ceremony, the students follow instructions to find their classrooms.

In Mambo's classroom, the teacher, Mr. Fonkou, announces the first lesson: **"Each of you will introduce yourself. Then we will learn a song about our body parts."**

When it is his turn, Mambo stands up and says, loudly

"My name is Mambo!"

After the introductions, Mr. Fonkou asks the class to repeat the body parts song after him:

This is my head,

That I touch with my hand!

This is my left ear,

That I touch with my right hand!

This is my right ear,

That I touch with my left hand!

Mambo and his classmates laugh as they get all tangled up in their own arms. Even the birds outside the window chirp joyfully.

This is my right foot,

That I touch with my left hand,

This is my left foot,

That I touch with my right hand!

When the bell rings for break time, Mambo and Kai reunite for lunch. They both share their food like best friends do. Mambo shares a banana in exchange for a piece of sandwich from Kai.

The bell rings once again at the end of the break. The students return to class. Mr. Fonkou asks, **"What have you learned today?"**

Mambo raises his hand in the air. "Pick me, sir; pick me, sir," he chants.

"Yes, Mambo," says Mr. Fonkou.

"I learned about left and right. It was so much fun," says Mambo.

The bell rings one more time to end the school day. Mambo and Kai reunite again. Together, they happily skip their way back to the village as they sing:

This is my head!
That I touch with my hand!
This is my left ear,
That I touch with my right hand!
This is my right ear,
That I touch with my left hand!
This is my right foot,
That I touch with my left hand,
This is my left foot,
That I touch with my right hand!

Mambo winks at Kai and says goodbye. Mambo cannot wait to sing his new funny song to his mother.

What a very special first day of school it has been! Mambo's mom was right:

Mambo really does like school very much.